Emmerly Finds Her Light

Story by Heather Mays

Illustrations by Elettra Cudignotto

For those who seek and honor the light within...

Emmerly woke up, opened her eyes and knew she was in a bad mood.

The sun was too bright. Her bed felt lumpy. The book she was reading the night before was crumpled and bent.

Her dog Sunny tried to cheer her up with kisses but even that didn't help. Looking around her room at all her treasured possessions, she couldn't find anything to make her smile.

It's a terrible thing to feel bad at the very start of the day!

Emmerly picked up her necklace from the bedside table, put on her slippers and shuffled down the hallway into the kitchen.

"What's wrong, sweetheart?" asked her Mom, seeing the sour expression on her face.

"I can't explain it," Emmerly answered. "I don't feel sick. I don't feel tired. I just feel less than I did yesterday. I feel small and sad and just...blah!"

Emmerly's mom pointed to the necklace on the table. "Look at your light," she said. "It's not as bright as it was yesterday. Sometimes, things happen around us that make us feel bad and we need to find our light again. When you shine brightly, you feel better and help others feel better too."

"Let's go to the zoo and see if your animal friends can teach you how to find your light again!"

The first animal Emmerly met at the zoo was Polar Bear.

"Excuse me, sir," she said. "I've lost some of my light. Could you help me learn how to find it again?"

Polar Bear replied, "You are a wise girl to look for your light! Sometimes the noise and activity around me can feel scary. People shout and jump around to get my attention and sometimes I want to shout back or hide so that they can't see me."

"But instead I listen to my breathing, my heartbeat and my own thoughts. We all have a song that plays within us, the song of ourselves that only we can hear. I tune out others and tune in to that song so I can hear and know myself. That's how I find my light when it is lost."

When she walked into the jungle, Emmerly noticed that one monkey was sitting by himself. She politely asked him, "Hi friend! I want to learn how to find my light that I have lost. Would you help me?"

"Yes!" replied Monkey. "With my arm in this sling, I can't swing on branches or run and play with my friends right now. I could be sad and feel that I'm missing out, but while the others are playing, I get to sit on this big, comfortable rock and drink my banana juice without worrying that I'll spill it."

"Sometimes when things don't go the way we want them to, we end up with something even better. Instead of feeling bad about what I don't have or what I can't do, I choose to love what I lack and that's how I find my light!"

Emmerly knew that Turtle would have some great advice.

"Beautiful friend, can you help me find my light?" she asked.

Turtle answered, "Sometimes, my friends talk and move too fast and I get left behind. I feel like I'm not welcome to join them when I can't keep up. It seems like I am alone with no one who understands me."

"But it can be fun to be alone. I get to notice all of the beauty around me when I go slower than everyone else. I can just be myself and not worry about fitting in with others."

Turtle continued, "I go at my own pace and that's how I find my light."

Emmerly introduced herself to Chameleon. He quickly changed the color of his skin to the brightest and most vibrant shades of green, yellow and orange!

"Little girl," he said gently, "I am sorry to hear that you've lost your light. Would you like to know what I do when that happens to me?"

"Oh yes!" said Emmerly. "I would love to learn from you!"

"In any moment, you can decide how to see the world around you. There are times when I see people fighting and times when it looks dark outside, but I choose to focus on sunshine and bright, bold colors. I find my light by choosing my view."

At Lion's house, Emmerly started to feel hungry.

"Come in and have something to eat," said Lion.

"Wow! Your home is so lovely," said Emmerly through a mouthful of cookie. "How is it that you have so many trophies and beautiful things?"

Lion answered, "When I'm having a bad day and I feel like I'm not shining as brightly as I normally do, I pretend that I have already won a contest, found a treasure or noticed a four-leaf clover. I expect great things to happen for me. I just know that they will! I live my luck and then I find that my light shines more brightly!"

Fox invited Emmerly to play a game of cards. Emmerly asked Fox, "How do you find your light when you don't feel like yourself?"

"I like to use my imagination!" said Fox.

"I pretend that I am playing a game of cards with a very good friend. I want to do all the things that make me believe in myself so that I can win the game and have a good time."

Emmerly replied, "That sounds like fun! Do you ever worry that you might lose your game?"

"I don't let myself think about the games I've lost in the past or the bad things that have happened to me. When I pretend to play my game, I bet on myself and I don't look back!"

As she walked to the next animal's home at the zoo, Emmerly heard a terrible clatter coming from behind one of the buildings. "Oh, Raccoon!" she exclaimed. "What a mess you've gotten yourself into!"

"It's not a mess, it's an adventure!" said Raccoon. "Would you like to look for your light in these bins? Maybe we can find it if we work together?"

"I'll just stand here," said Emmerly, not wanting to get dirty.

Raccoon laughed. "Trash really isn't so bad, you know! Sometimes it can feel like the odds are stacked against us, like these trash cans, filled with bad and smelly stuff. The best thing to do is to climb over and out and not worry so much. When you have fun, you will find your light!"

Emmerly walked slowly into Bear's woods, not wanting to startle anyone she may meet there.

Bear invited her over to the campfire. "Here, sweet child. Have a snack while you sit down and rest."

"Thank you!" said Emmerly. "It has been a busy day already and I'm a little tired. Everyone has taught me such wonderful things, but I feel like it may be too hard to find my light again. It seems like a lot of work."

"Finding your light isn't always easy," Bear said. "Life can be messy like melted chocolate and sticky marshmallows! When we understand that our challenges can teach us how to do better and how to be better, we find and shine our light."

Coming out of Bear's woods, Emmerly saw a colorful flower garden. The sunshine made her happy and she started to twirl around and dance.

She heard a tiny voice laughing and saw that Bee was flying toward her. "Hello, little friend!" Emmerly said. "You live in such a beautiful place! I bet you never lose your light!"

"It helps to see things with a positive attitude," said Bee. "Some people think that the flower you're holding is a weed and that it doesn't belong in the garden, but dandelions have a special job of carrying our wishes out into the world. When we see something as a wish and not a weed, we understand that Life can be a magical adventure. That's how I find and shine my light!"

Elephant was having her afternoon tea when Emmerly arrived.

"Please serve yourself, dear," Elephant said. "The teapot is full and there is an empty cup on the table."

Emmerly poured tea into her cup, careful not to spill any on the tablecloth. It was hard but she felt proud that she was able to do it herself. She asked Elephant, "You look so happy and calm. What lesson can you share with me about finding my light?"

"I have learned that it's up to each of us to fill our own cup and take care of ourselves. When you understand that you control your own actions and your own feelings, you find and shine your light."

Emmerly was excited to meet Owl. She knew that Owl was wise and could teach her an important lesson.

"Beautiful friend," Emmerly whispered, for Owl was just waking up. "I have learned so many lessons today and I would love to hear your advice for finding and shining my light. What can you teach me?"

Owl yawned, stretched and blinked her eyes before answering. "I decide not to hide my light, even when it feels dark around me. Each day, I rise up and I stand tall and proud. I know that my light can help others feel good about themselves, so I don't hide it. Being confident and brave is how I find and shine my light."

Emmerly climbed the ladder in Giraffe's yard so that she could speak to him face-to-face. Everything looked very different from high up in the tree.

"You must have a very big light to shine since you are so tall. How do you keep from losing it?" Emmerly asked.

"I understand that I am very different from my friends and that I can see things in my own way. I know that I am unique. I don't say something simply because someone else says it. I don't do something just because it's what everyone else does. Each of us is special just the way we are. I know that I wasn't made to be like everyone else. That's how I find and shine my light – by standing out and not trying to fit in!"

Back in her bed that evening, Emmerly thought about all that she had learned.   Her light was beaming and she felt so much better. She felt like herself again!

Sunny the dog jumped off the bed, circled around on the rug and settled in for a night of dreaming about squirrels. As she drifted off to sleep, Sunny heard Emmerly say,

"I know that when I don't feel like myself, my light is shining less brightly than it could. I can follow the steps my animal friends shared with me to find my light again and feel better."

"I can't wait to wake up tomorrow and shine my light!"

The End

Parents and Teachers

For related activities and discussion prompts, visit
http://www.emmerlyfindsherlight.com

The 12 steps mentioned within these pages are based on concepts introduced in the book Hey Radiant Souls: A Guide for Finding and Shining Your Light, available here:
http://www.heyradiantsouls.com

The Steps:
Tune Out to Tune In
Love What You Lack
Embrace Your Pace
Choose Your View
Live Your Luck
Bet on Yourself & Don't Look Back
The Odds May Be Stacked Against You
Expect S'More
Weed or Wish
Fill Your Own Cup
Rise Up and Shine
Stand Out - You Weren't Made to Fit In

About the Author

Heather Mays is an Intuitive Counselor, Animal Communicator, Artist and Photographer. She is on a mission to empower and embolden others to connect with their Divine Radiant Light and to honor the sacred connection with all Life.

Learn more about Heather: http://www.heathermays.com

About the Illustrator .

Elettra Cudignotto is an artist and illustrator based in Italy.

Learn more about Elettra: http://www.elettracudignotto.com

Made in the USA
Monee, IL
19 December 2021

86389833R00024